ABOUT PIXAR ANIMATION STUDIOS
ARTIST SHOWCASE BOOKS

This series of original picture books puts the spotlight on the
incredible artists of Pixar Animation Studios. The pages of each
book showcase the personal work of one of these talented artists
and introduce a brand-new world and characters.

For Dad, whose strength and wisdom have
weathered every storm. For Adam, thank you for
your humor and warm heart. And for Mom,
whose long journey has inspired me to stay strong.

Kampung \ ˈkäm-poŋ \: village

Sayang \ ˈsā-ˈ jæŋ\: dear

Inshallah \ ˌin-shä-ˈlä \: God willing

Assalamu alaikum \ əs-sə-ˈlä-mü-ə-ˈlī-kúm \: peace be upon you

First Hardcover Edition, April 2019
10 9 8 7 6 5 4 3 2 1
FAC-029191-19004
ISBN 978-1-368-01590-5
Printed in Malaysia

This book is set in Halewyn and Mandolin.
Designed by Scott Piehl.
Illustrations created digitally.

Library of Congress Control Number: 2018033419

Reinforced binding
Visit www.disneybooks.com

PIXAR ANIMATION STUDIOS ARTIST SHOWCASE

Mommy Sayang

Rosana Sullivan

D̲ISNE̲Y PRESS

Los Angeles · New York

In a small village—a *kampung*—
past the rice paddy fields...

...filled with **chicks** and **chickens**

and **cats** and **kittens**...

...lived **little Aleeya** and her dear mommy—
Mommy *sayang*.

Five times a day,

Mommy *sayang* prayed,
while **Aleeya** lay close by her side.

Together, chores were never a bore,

whether watering the **red hibiscus flowers**

or stirring up the **spiciest** recipes.

At meals with **family** and **friends**, Aleeya watched the dance of dishes from her seat on **Mommy's** lap.

In the evenings, **Aleeya** would lie under the mosquito net, listening to **Mommy** *sayang*'s stories.

Before drifting off to sleep, Aleeya would ask, "Mommy *sayang*, will you always be by my side?"

"*Inshallah*, Aleeya *sayang*, I will always be by your side," Mommy would reply, with a kiss on Aleeya's forehead.

In Aleeya's favorite dream, she and Mommy tumbled together among endless fields of flowers.

With a **WHOOSH** of their magic power, out
would pop an enormous **hibiscus flower**!

Under the shade of the **red petals**, they would
munch on crispy curry puffs...

...until the dream flickered and faded
to a new tomorrow.

One day, Mommy *sayang*
was not feeling okay.

Aleeya waited and waited...

...and waited,

but **Mommy** still was not better.

"Come join us for a walk," Aleeya's aunties
would say, but she refused.

Aleeya only wanted Mommy.

So **Aleeya** sat alone, day after day, wrapped tightly in **Mommy's** sarong.

One morning, the meow of a kitten made **Aleeya** look up.

There in a pot was a **red hibiscus**, almost as big as the one in her dream.

The flower gave her an idea.

Skipping up steps and hopping down the hall,
Aleeya climbed onto Mommy *sayang*'s bed.

Aleeya gently placed the flower in Mommy's hands, kissed her forehead, and said,

"Mommy *sayang*, *Inshallah*, I will always be by your side."

And little by little, with Aleeya's help...

...Mommy felt better.

Assalamu alaikum!

My name is Rosana,

but you can call me Rosie.

When I was little, I used to watch my mom paint pictures of her
kampung (which means "village") in Malaysia.

This inspired me to draw on any piece of paper I could find,

including my dad's biology exam papers!

When my mom became really ill, drawing became my outlet and comfort.

I would create fantastic stories and characters that I could relate to,

and together my mom and I shared our mutual love of storytelling and art.

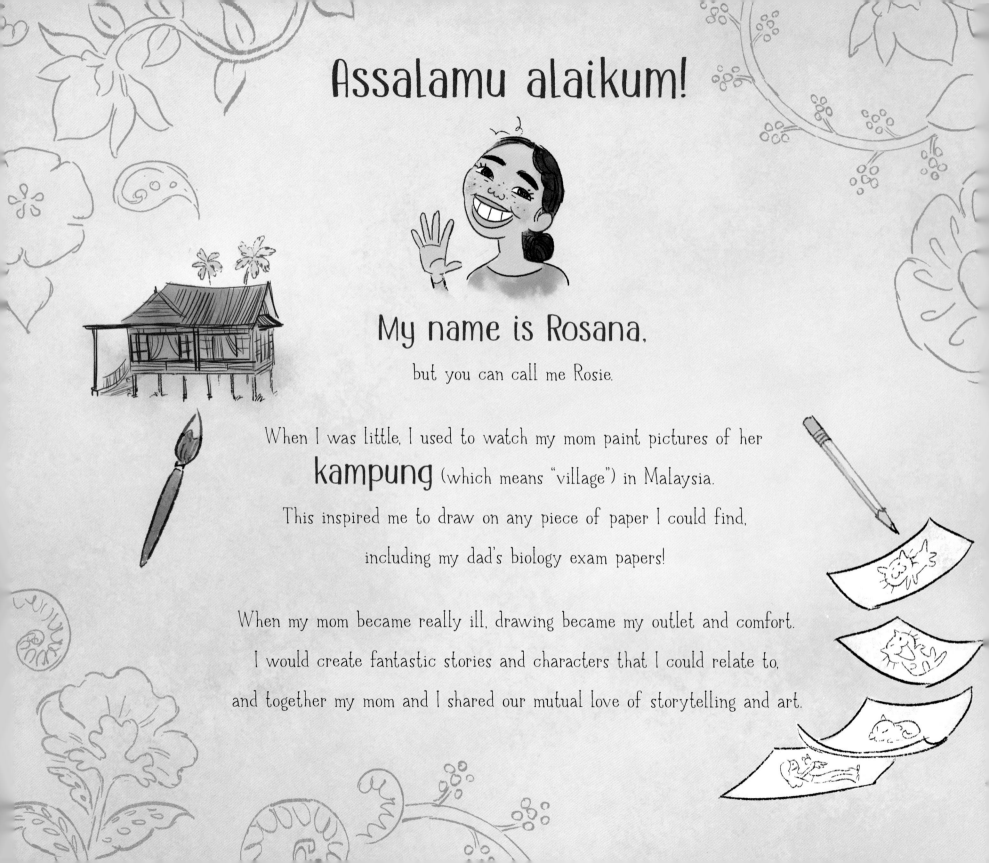

Even though I loved art, I initially studied to become a veterinarian.
However, a painting teacher saw how passionate I was about art,
and she encouraged me to apply for an internship at Pixar.

But it was not so easy!

After graduating from the University of San Francisco, I knew I had
to have a strong portfolio. So I enrolled at the Academy of Art
and worked very hard at improving my drawing skills.

Finally, I was hired at Pixar in 2011 as a story artist! I got to work on
many films, such as *The Good Dinosaur*, *Coco*, and *Incredibles 2*.
I even got to direct my own 2-D animated short, *Kitbull*.

Now that I have a son, I hope to draw more stories
that I can share with my Otto *sayang*
(that means "dear") as he grows up!